W9-CBX-915

Henry Bear's Christmas

Atheneum Books for Young Readers

An imprint of Simon & Schuster Children's Publishing Division

1230 Avenue of the Americas

New York, New York 10020

Copyright © 2003 by David McPhail

All rights reserved, including the right of reproduction in whole or in part in any form.

Book design by Kristin Smith

The text of this book was set in Bembo.

The illustrations were rendered in crow-quill pen, ink, and watercolor.

Manufactured in China

First Edition

2 4 6 8 10 9 7 5 3 1

Library of Congress Cataloging-in-Publication Data

McPhail, David M.

Henry Bear's Christmas / David McPhail.—1st ed.

p.   cm.

Summary: Henry Bear is determined to win the raffle for the perfect Christmas tree so
he will not even consider his friend Stanley's choice of trees.

ISBN 0-689-82198-0

[1. Bears—Fiction. 2. Raccoons—Fiction. 3. Christmas trees—Fiction.

4. Christmas—Fiction.]

PZ7 .M2427 Hd 2001

[E]—dc21   00-042018

Henry Bear's Christmas

written and illustrated by david mcphail

coloring by john o'connor

atheneum books for young readers

NEW YORK • LONDON • TORONTO • SYDNEY • SINGAPORE

It was the first day of December. Henry Bear knew for sure that it was, because he had run out of numbers on the calendar to check off on his countdown to Christmas.

Henry loved Christmas. Oh, to be sure, he loved Christmas for all the presents, and for all the good food—especially the extra jelly cakes that Momma Bear always baked at Christmastime.

But Christmas was even more—a special time of love and warmth and good cheer, when even strangers smiled and said, "Merry Christmas!" Then there was the singing and the sleigh rides and the ice skating on the pond with big mugs of hot cider afterward to warm the tummy.

Perhaps, though, the thing Henry loved most about Christmas was the tree. A fine and full Christmas tree, beautifully decorated, with presents underneath and good friends all around. That was Christmas, all right—and Henry smiled as he thought about it.

"Today is the first day of December," Henry said to Stanley. "It's time we started looking for a tree."

"But Christmas is still more than a fortnight away," protested Stanley. "We've got plenty of time!"

"Nothing of the sort," said Henry. "If we don't start looking right away, all the best trees will be taken—there's not a moment to lose!" And he put on his hat, scarf, and gloves.

Stanley knew it would be futile to argue further, so he slipped into his imitation raccoon coat and followed Henry down the ladder.

As they walked to town, Stanley could see that
Henry was right about all the best trees being taken.
There were people everywhere carrying trees or
loading them onto sleds and pulling them home.

The first place they came to where trees were being sold was the farm stand. FRESH CUT ON THE PREMISES, read a large, roughly lettered sign. There were a great many trees here, all sizes and shapes, but not one with the size and shape to suit Henry.

Next they went to the school yard, where students were selling trees to benefit their scholarship fund.

Henry and Stanley walked around, examining each tree carefully. "This just won't do!" Henry said about each tree they examined.

They were about to leave, when Stanley spotted a tree lying off by itself in a corner of the school yard.

Pulling his sleeve, Stanley coaxed Henry to where the tree lay half buried in the snow. Stanley reached down and lifted the tree gently and stood it upright. "How about this one?" he asked Henry.

Henry scowled. "That is the scrawniest, most pathetic-looking tree I've ever seen!" he said. "Half the branches are missing, and the needles have already turned brown!"

"I like it," Stanley said softly.

"Let's try the church," Henry said enthusiastically. "They always have good trees."

This year the church had one tree, but it was a beautiful tree, a perfect tree; even Stanley had to admit it was the most beautiful tree he had ever seen.

"How much?" Henry asked the vicar as he pulled his money pouch from his pocket.

"It's not for sale," replied the vicar. "It's being raffled off. The person with the winning ticket takes it away!"

"How much are the tickets?" Henry persisted.

"Fifty cents for one," the vicar answered. "Three for a dollar."

Henry took all of his Christmas tree money from his pocket and counted it out. "Three dollars and seventy cents," he said as he handed it to the vicar. "How many tickets will that buy?"

"Let's call it an even dozen," said the vicar "Good luck, and a Merry Christmas to you, too."

"Oh, boy," Henry said to Stanley on the return trip home. "I just know we're gonna win that tree!"

"But the vicar said they've sold hundreds of tickets," Stanley pointed out, "and we only have twelve!"

"Even if we had just one," Henry replied confidently, for he truly believed that he was meant to have that tree, "I know that I'd still win!"

"I still think that we should have bought the one at the school yard," mumbled Stanley. "At least we'd have a tree for sure."

But nothing could shake Henry's firm belief that the tree was as good as his.

At supper that evening the raffle was all Henry could talk about. He rearranged the furniture in the living room and left a big space for "his" tree. He carved some new tree decorations, and made yards of paper chains.

The night before the winning ticket was to be drawn was a sleepless one for Henry. He tossed and turned while visions of "his" tree danced through his dreams. In one dream the tree was wearing wings, and growing smaller and smaller as Henry walked toward it.

"What do you suppose that means?" Henry asked Stanley after telling him about his dream as they walked toward the church.

"Search me," answered Stanley. He had a pretty good idea what it all meant, but was hesitant to say.

As they passed the school yard Stanley noticed that the tree
he liked was still there—off by itself.

"There's my tree," he said to Henry. "I still think we should
have bought that one."

"You'll forget all about *that* tree," Henry assured him, "when
I win my tree."

At the church there were dozens of people standing around waiting for the vicar to appear. All of them were hopeful of winning the tree, but none as hopeful as Henry, who was hopping from one foot to the other, as much in excited anticipation as in an effort to keep warm in the chilly winter air.

"I'm freezing!" Henry said to Stanley. "I'm going across the street to the doughnut shop for a mug of cocoa."

"But what if the vicar comes while you're gone?" Stanley asked nervously.

"He won't," said Henry. "Besides, I'll be right back." And he pushed through the crowd and walked over to the doughnut shop.

Henry had no sooner stepped inside the doughnut shop when the vicar appeared, carrying a large basket filled with the stubs of raffle tickets. The vicar stepped into the crowd and asked an old man to reach into the basket and draw one out.

The old man removed a mitten and shoved his hand deep into the basket. He pulled out a stub and handed it to the vicar.

"The winning number is eighty-nine!" the vicar called out. "Is the lucky owner of number eighty-nine here?" There was no reply.

"I repeat," said the vicar. "Will the person holding the ticket number eighty-nine please step forward!"

Still no response.

"If the possessor of raffle ticket number eighty-nine does

not step forward within the next two minutes," the vicar persisted, "we shall have to draw another number!"

"I wonder if Henry has number eighty-nine," Stanley said to himself. "Where is he, anyway?"

Stanley looked around, trying to see if Henry was on his way back from the doughnut shop. Finding that his view was blocked by the crowd of people pressing close behind him, Stanley decided to go and hurry Henry along.

When Stanley finally got to the doughnut shop, sure enough, there was Henry, sitting at the counter, a steaming mug of cocoa in front of him and his mouth stuffed with doughnuts.

"The drawing has already been made!" puffed Stanley. "Number eighty-nine is the winner!"

Henry sputtered and coughed, and nearly choked. "I've got number eighty-nine!" he cried happily. "I won!"

"Not yet, you haven't," Stanley told him. "The vicar gave you two minutes to claim your tree, and that two minutes is very nearly up!"

Henry gulped down his cocoa and his last bite of doughnut. "Honeydip," he remarked, smacking his lips. Then he dashed out the door behind Stanley.

Henry and Stanley got across the street just in time to hear the vicar announce, "The new winning ticket number is one hundred five!"

Henry charged through the crowd, waving his ticket. "Number eighty-nine," he shouted. "I've got number eighty-nine!"

Henry reached the vicar a second or two after the holder of ticket number 105 had laid claim on the tree and was already dragging it off.

"My tree!" Henry squealed. "I'm number eighty-nine!"

"Too late," the vicar told Henry. "You had two minutes to claim your tree, and the two minutes were up long ago!"

Henry was crushed. He had known from the start that he would win that tree. And he had, in a way. Well, sort of.

All of a sudden Henry began to feel a little foolish. He had

spent all of the Christmas tree money on those raffle tickets, and now they had no money left to buy a tree. But then he thought some more. "We can still buy a tree!" said Henry. "We can use the grocery money!"

"No, we can't," Stanley said meekly. "It's all gone!"

"All gone?" Henry said, puzzled.

"Yes," explained Stanley. "I spent it on raffle tickets for *'your'* tree. I knew how much that tree meant to you, so I took the grocery money and bought some more tickets."

Henry just groaned. Then he began to chuckle. Pretty soon he was laughing so hard that he fell right over into the snow.

Stanley couldn't help smiling. "What's so funny?" he asked.

"Us!" roared Henry, holding his sides for the pain his laughter was causing him. "First we have no tree, and now we have no Christmas dinner, either!"

Stanley still didn't see the humor in it, but Henry's laughter was so infectious that before long he was laughing and stumbling around too.

After awhile, Stanley helped Henry to his feet, and arm in arm the two friends staggered home.

They were crossing through the school yard when they noticed that the students were preparing to close for the night.

The students were dragging the unsold trees into an enclosed area where they would be locked in until the next day. One of the students was closing the gate when Stanley noticed that "his" tree, the scrawny, brown-needled one, was still lying in one corner of the yard.

"You forgot one," Stanley called to the students, and he pointed to the pathetic little tree.

"We don't want that one," a student replied.

"Can we have it then?" Stanley asked excitedly.

"Help yourself," they said.

So Stanley ran to the tree and stood it up in the snow.

Henry walked around the tree three times before he spoke. "Now that I look at it more closely," he observed. "I see that it's not such a bad little tree after all."

Stanley breathed a sigh of relief and squeezed Henry's arm. "Thanks," he said. "At least now we have a Christmas tree."

Henry chuckled. "And who knows," he said. "Maybe Momma Bear will bring us some Christmas dinner, too!"

And she did, . . .

with red-and-green jelly cakes for dessert.

DISCARDED

PEACHTREE

J PICTURE MCPHAIL   PTREE
McPhail, David
Henry Bear's Christmas

NOV 13 2003

Atlanta-Fulton Public Library